First published 1980 by
Octopus Books Limited
59 Grosvenor Street
London W1

Second impression, 1982

© 1980 Octopus Books Limited

ISBN 0 7064 1360 1

Produced by Mandarin Publishers Limited
22a Westland Road, Quarry Bay, Hong Kong

Printed in Hong Kong

Educational and Series advisor Felicia Law

PDO 81-945

Nursery Rhymes

compiled by
Suzanne Chandler

illustrated by
Diane Tippell

octopus

A Treasure Trove of
Traditional Nursery Rhymes

Girls and boys
Three little kittens
The Queen of Hearts
Sing a song of sixpence
Baa baa black sheep
Ride a cock horse
Little Polly Flinders
Up wooden hill
Lavender's blue
Kindness
Barber, barber
Wee little house
The Grand Old Duke of York
Humpty Dumpty
The lion and the unicorn
Wee Willie Winkie
Old King Cole
Simple Simon
Hey diddle diddle

Little Miss Muffet
Tweedle dum and
  Tweedle dee
Algy met a bear
The North wind
Eency, weency spider
Higgledy piggledy
  my black hen
Six little mice
Jack Sprat
Hickory, dickory, dock
Diddle, diddle, dumpling
Twinkle, twinkle
An old woman
Which is the way
There was a crooked man
Cock a doodle doo!
Higgledy piggledy
I had a little nut tree

Girls and boys

Girls and boys come out to play,
The moon doth shine as bright as day.
Leave your supper and leave your sleep,
And come with your playfellows into the street.
Come with a whoop and come with a call,
Come with a good will or not at all.
Up the ladder and down the wall,
A halfpenny loaf will serve us all;
You find milk and I'll find flour,
and we'll have a pudding in half an hour.

Three little kittens

Three little kittens they lost their mittens,
  And they began to cry,
Oh, mother dear, we sadly fear
  That we have lost our mittens.
What! lost your mittens, you naughty kittens!
  Then you shall have no pie.
  Mee-ow, mee-ow, mee-ow.
  No, you shall have no pie.

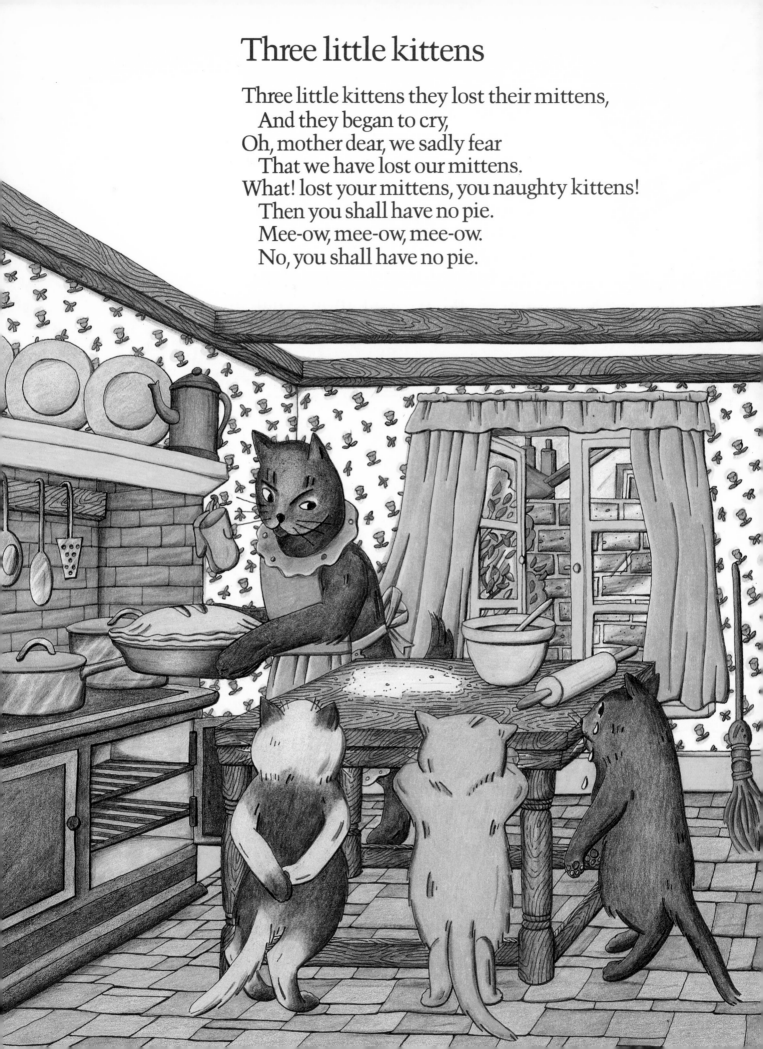

The three little kittens they found their mittens,
    And they began to cry,
Oh, mother dear, see here, see here,
    For we have found our mittens.
Put on your mittens, you silly kittens,
    And you shall have some pie.
    Purr-r, purr-r, purr-r,
    Oh, let us have some pie.

The Queen of Hearts

The Queen of Hearts
She made some tarts;
All on a summer's day;
The Knave of Hearts
He stole those tarts
And took them clean away

The King of Hearts
Called for those tarts
And beat the knave full sore;
The Knave of Hearts
Brought back those tarts,
And vowed he'd steal no more.

Sing a song of sixpence

Sing a song of sixpence,
    A pocket full of rye;
Four and twenty blackbirds,
    Baked in a pie.
When the pie was opened,
    The birds began to sing;
Now wasn't that a dainty dish,
    To set before the king?

Baa, baa, black sheep

Baa, baa, black sheep,
  Have you any wool?
Yes sir, yes sir
  Three bags full;
One for the master,
  And one for the dame,
And one for the little boy
  Who lives down the lane.

Ride a cock horse

Ride a cock horse to Banbury Cross,
To see a fine lady ride on a white horse;
Rings on her fingers and bells on her toes,
And she shall have music wherever she goes.

Little Polly Flinders

Little Polly Flinders
Sat among the cinders,
Warming her pretty little toes;
Her mother came and caught her,
And scolded her daughter
For spoiling her nice new clothes.

Up wooden hill

Up wooden hill,
Down sheet lane,
Cross pillow bank
And here we are again.

Lavender's blue

Lavender's blue, dilly, dilly,
   Lavender's green;
When I am king, dilly, dilly,
   You shall be queen.
Lavender's green, dilly, dilly,
   Lavender's blue,
If you love me, dilly, dilly,
   I shall love you.

Kindness

I love little pussy,
    Her coat is so warm,
And if I don't hurt her
    She'll do me no harm.
I'll not pull her tail,
    Nor drive her away,
And pussy and I
    together will play.

Barber, barber

Barber, barber, shave a pig,
How many hairs will make a wig?
Four and twenty that's enough.
Give the barber a pinch of snuff.

Wee little house

Wee little house with the golden thatch;
Twice I knocked and I lifted the latch:
"And pray, is the mistress here?"
"In black stuff gown and a yellow vest,
She's busily packing her honey-chest;
Will you taste a bit, my dear?"

The Grand Old Duke of York

Oh, the Grand Old Duke of York,
  He had ten thousand men;
He marched them up to the top of the hill
  And he marched them down again.
And when they were up they were up,
  And when they were down, they were down,
And when they were only half way up,
  They were neither up nor down.

Humpty Dumpty

Humpty Dumpty sat on a wall,
Humpty Dumpty had a great fall,
All the king's horses and all the king's men
Couldn't put Humpty together again.

The lion and the unicorn

The lion and the unicorn
  Fought for the crown;
The lion beat the unicorn
  Up and down the town.

Some gave them white bread,
  And some gave them brown;
Some gave them plum cake
  And sent them out of town.

Wee Willie Winkie

Wee Willie Winkie runs throught the town,
Upstairs and downstairs in his nightgown,
Rapping at the window, crying at the lock,
Are the children all in bed, it's past eight o'clock?

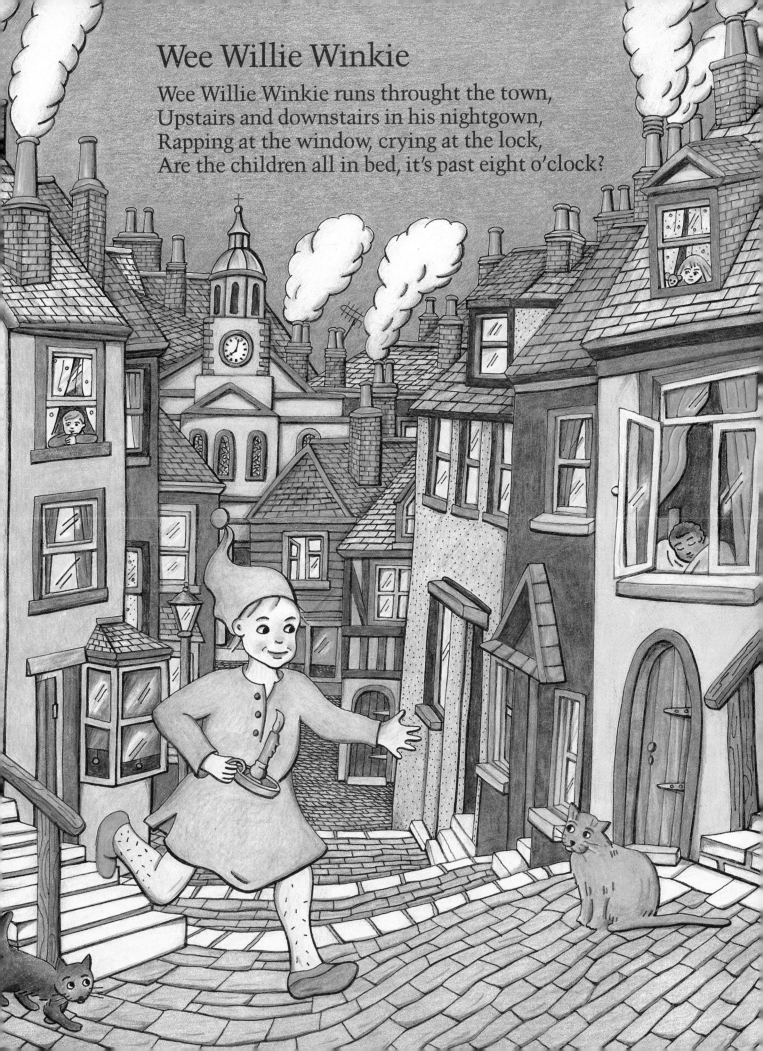

Old King Cole

Old King Cole
Was a merry old soul,
And a merry old soul was he;
He called for his pipe,
And he called for his bowl,
And he called for his fiddlers three.

Every fiddler he had a fiddle
And a very fine fiddle had he;
   Oh, there's none so rare
   As can compare
With King Cole and his fiddlers three.

Simple Simon

Simple Simon met a pieman
    Going to the Fair;
Said Simple Simon to the pieman,
    Let me taste your ware.

Said the pieman unto Simon,
    Show me first your penny;
Said Simple Simon to the pieman
    Sir, I have not any.

Hey diddle diddle

Hey diddle diddle,
The cat and the fiddle,
The cow jumped over the moon;
The little dog laughed
To see such fun,
And the dish ran away with the spoon

Little Miss Muffet

Little Miss Muffet
Sat on her tuffet,
Eating her curds and whey;
There came a GREAT spider,
Who sat down beside her
And frightened Miss Muffet away.

Tweedle dum and Tweedle dee

Tweedle dum and Tweedle dee
    resolved to have a battle.
For Tweedle dum said Tweedle dee
    had spoiled his nice new rattle.
Just then flew by a monstrous crow,
As big as a tar barrel,
Which frightened both the heroes so
    They quite forgot their quarrel.

Algy met a bear

Algy met a bear,
A bear met Algy.
The bear was bulgy,
The bulge was Algy.

The North wind

The North wind doth blow,
And we shall have snow,
And what will the Robin do then?
   Poor thing
He'll sit in a barn,
And keep himself warm,
And tuck his head under his wing,
   Poor thing.

Eency, weency spider

Eency, weency spider
Climbed the water spout;
Down came the rain
And washed poor spider out.

Out came the sunshine
And dried up the rain.
Eency, weency spider
Climbed up again.

Higgledy piggledy my black hen

Higgledy, piggledy my black hen,
She lays eggs for gentlemen.
Sometimes nine and sometimes ten,
Higgledy, piggledy my black hen.

Six little mice

Six little mice sat down to spin;
Pussy passed by and she peeped in.
What are you doing, my little men?
Weaving coats for gentlemen.
Shall I come in and cut off your threads?
No, no Mistress Pussy, you'd bite off our heads.
Oh, no, I'll not; I'll help you to spin.
That may be so, but you don't come in.

Jack Sprat

Jack Sprat could eat no fat,
    His wife could eat no lean,
And so between the two of them,
    They kept the platter clean.

Hickory, dickory, dock

Hickory, dickory, dock,
The mouse ran up the clock.
  The clock struck one,
  The mouse ran down,
Hickory, dickory, dock.

Diddle, diddle, dumpling

Diddle, diddle, dumpling, my son John,
Went to bed with his trousers on;
One shoe off, and one shoe on
Diddle, diddle, dumpling, my son John.

Twinkle, twinkle

Twinkle, twinkle, little star,
How I wonder what you are!
Up above the sky so high,
Like a diamond in the sky.
Twinkle, twinkle, little star,
How I wonder what you are!

An old woman

There was an old woman toss'd up in a basket,
    Ninety times as high as the moon;
Where she was going, I couldn't but ask it,
    For in her hand she carried a broom.

Old woman, old woman, old woman, quoth I,
O whither, O whither, O whither so high?
To brush the cobwebs off the sky!
Shall I go with thee? Aye, by and by.

Which is the way

Which is the way to Somewhere
  Town?
Oh up in the morning early
Over the hills and the chimney pots
That is the way quite clearly.

And which is the door to Somewhere
  Town?
Oh up in the morning early
The round red sun is the door to go
  through
That is the way quite clearly.

There was a crooked man

There was a crooked man
   And he went a crooked mile
He found a crooked sixpence
   Against a crooked stile

He brought a crooked cat
   Which caught a crooked mouse
And they all lived together
   In a crooked little house.

Cock a doodle doo!

Cock a doodle doo!
My dame has lost her shoe,
My master's lost his fiddling stick,
And knows not what to do,

Cock a doodle doo!
My dame has found her shoe,
And master's found his fiddling stick,
Cock a doodle doo!

Cock a doodle doo!
My dame shall dance with you,
My master's found his fiddling stick,
Cock a doodle doo!

Higgledy piggledy

Higgledy piggledy see how they run,
Hopperty popperty what is the fun.
Has the sun or moon tumbled into the sea?
What is the matter pray tell me?

Higgledy piggledy how can I tell,
Hopperty popperty hark to the bell.
The rats and the mice even scamper away,
Who can say what may not happen today?

I had a little nut tree

I had a little nut tree,
    And nothing would it bear
But a silver nutmeg
    And a golden pear;
The King of Spain's daughter
    Came to visit me,
And all for the sake
    Of my little nut tree.
I skipped over water,
    I stepped over sea,
And all the birds in the air
    Couldn't catch me.